STICK IN THE MUD

Sir Charlie Brown

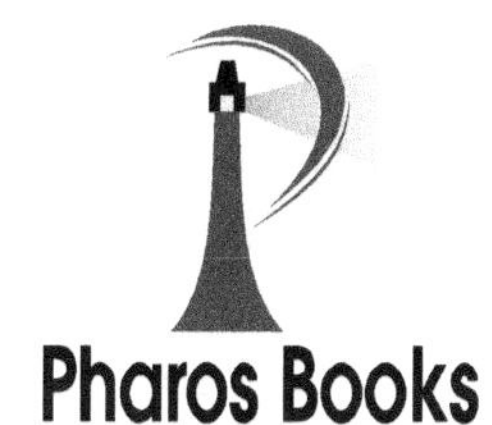

Pharos Books

ISBN: 978-93-91476-83-0
eISBN: 978-93-91476-91-5

© **Publishers**

Publisher: Pharos Books (P) Ltd.
Plot No.-55, Main Mother Dairy Road
Pandav Nagar, East Delhi-110092 (India)
Phone: +014049995474
WhatsApp: +014049995474
E-mail: sales@pharosbooks.in
Website: www.pharosbooks.in
Edition: 2021

STICK IN THE MUD
Author: Sir Charlie Brown

Cell phones mostly do communication these days. Thus making and fixing telephone poles seem obsolete. But there was a time, not long ago, when these huge poles were useful to the world. They were considered to be an important part of life. So, let me tell you a story of a logging truck that turned off the main highway onto a dirty road carrying a tall Telephone Pole into the forest.

Arriving at a clearing, the Pole had noticed that a hole had been dug in the ground for him.

"Is that for me?" the Pole wondered. He didn't have to wait long

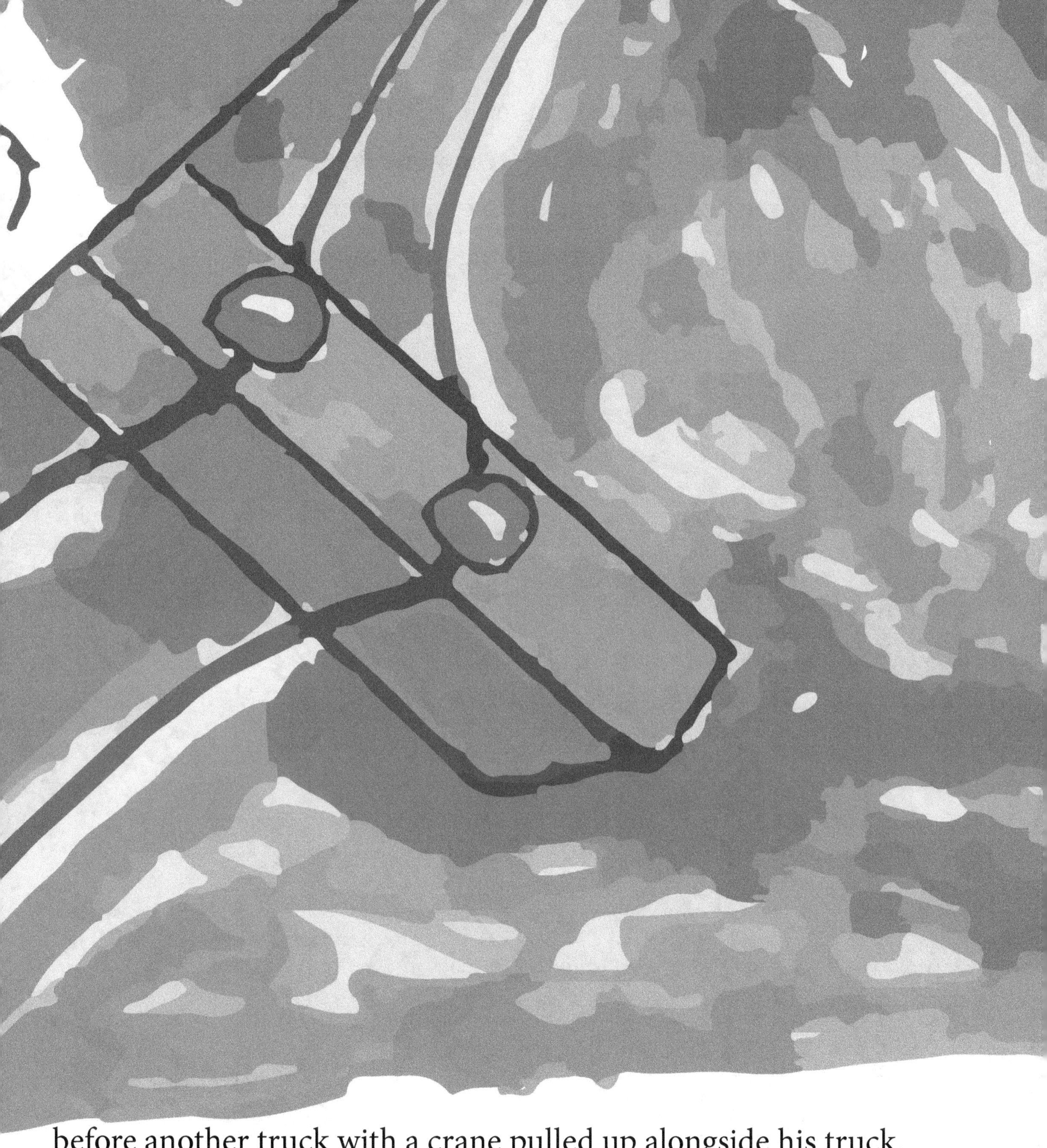

before another truck with a crane pulled up alongside his truck.

Soon the Pole felt light weight as he was lifted off the flatbed truck and put in place in the ground.

The forest was unusually quiet. Gradually, the maintenance guys returned and put arms on the Telephone Pole. Soon after, four cables, that stretched from pole to pole were connected to its arms. Soon, it got pretty boring just standing there in that hole.

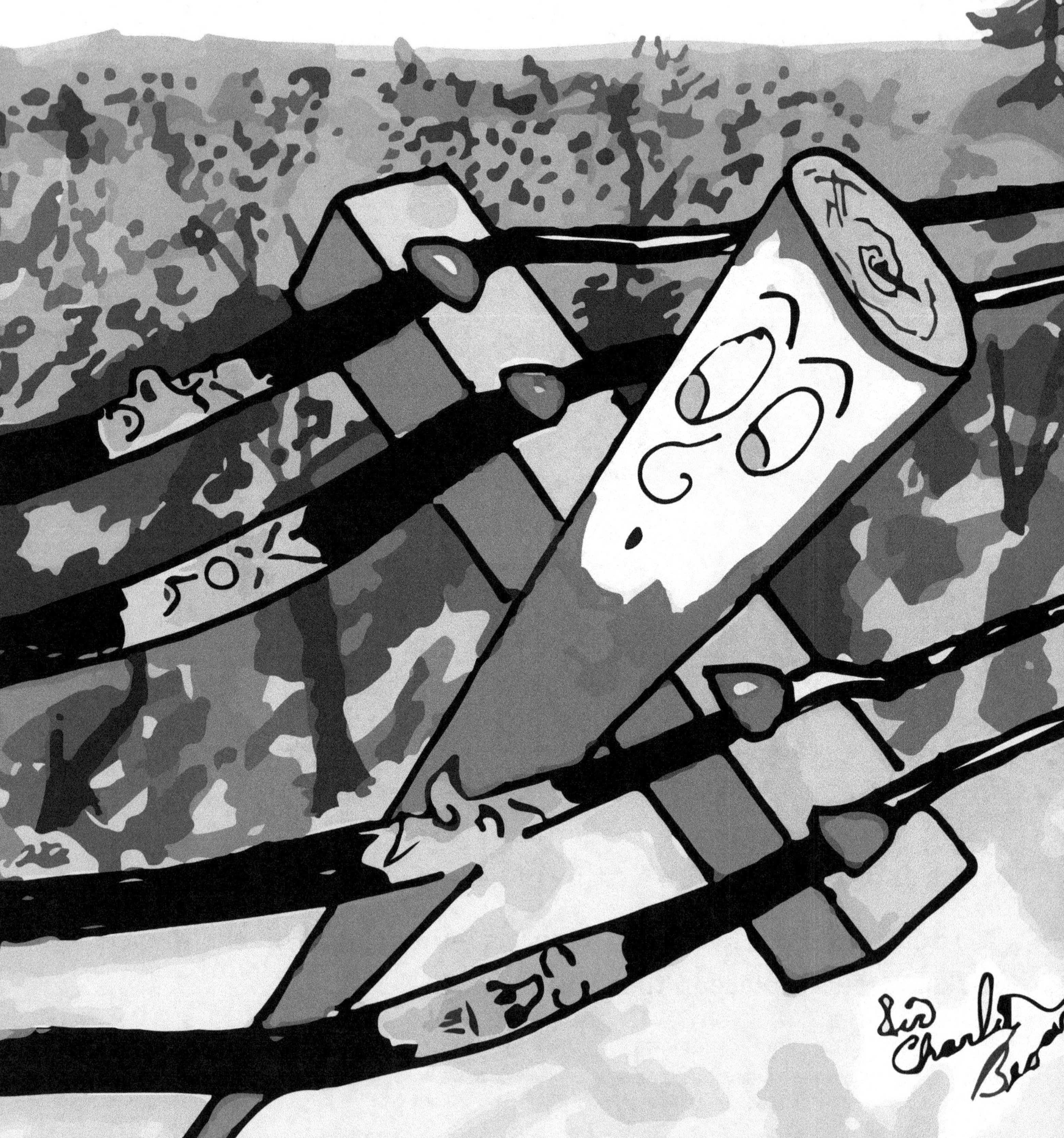

It was wonderful to have new neighbors, referring to the cables he now held to his arms. He tried to talk with them by saying "Hi!" But all the four cables seemed to ignore his kind gesture.

He tried several more times to talk with them, but to no avail.

Even though he tried as hard as he could, the cables would not talk to him. In fact, they snubbed him many times. The Pole then set his eyes on the local critters that passed by him. Even they were too

busy for him, because they were only looking for food and were not interested being friends with him.

Many times the Pole tried to talk with the four cables but the same thing happened. Finally, one of the cables became very irritated. It asked, "what is it you want?"

"I need a friend," the Pole replied.

"Well don't look for it around here," snapped the cable. "We only deal with the well-to-do, and we send messages to people living in the world. And you are not important enough to bother us. You're a no-body, you're nothing, you're just a stick in the mud. So don't talk to us, unless you have something important to say."

Deeply hurt by the way the cables spoke to him the Pole was sad.

Seasons changed rapidly and summer was now over. The cold chilly weather changing the trees to different colors from green to reds and oranges. The animals of the forest too were busy finding a place to hibernate until spring came around next year.

None of the animals told the Pole goodbye. Yet the Telephone Pole overlooked their intentions with an understanding that at least they weren't snubbing him.

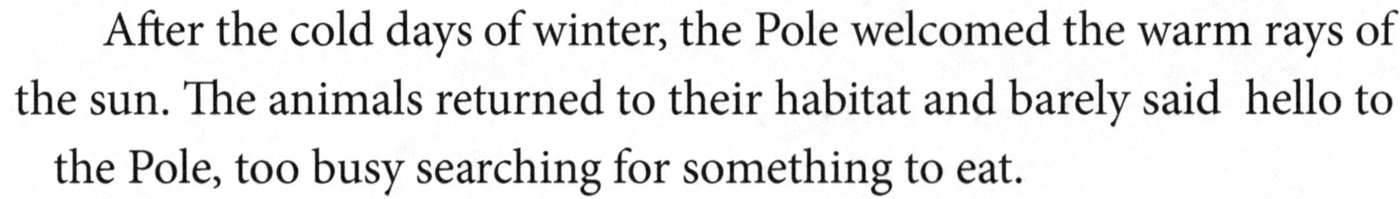

After the cold days of winter, the Pole welcomed the warm rays of the sun. The animals returned to their habitat and barely said hello to the Pole, too busy searching for something to eat.

But the Pole enjoyed watching them anyway. The cables were busy too, sending important messages to the world. Indeed, how lonely it was to live life… all alone.

Winter followed the chilly days of fall with much colder days. The temperature dropped below zero degree and the Pole standing

where he was, tried to talk to the cables, but once again they reminded him that he wasn't important to be talked to.

Summer was back again and a full year had gone by for the Pole. He had tried as hard as he might, but nothing he knew of would make him important enough for the four cables to at least speak to him.

This summer was unusually hot, and not only the animals but also plants and trees had a hard time getting water.

The Pole made another attempt to talk with the cables. "It's so hot would you like to have a little juice?"

"No!" they snapped. "Have you anything important to tell us?"

"No," the Pole said.

"How dare you talk to us then? Go back to where you came from, you 'stick in the mud!'"

The Pole drew back sadly and thought, "How can I tell them anything important when I am stuck here in this stupid hole in the ground.

Summer was over. Oh so soon! And the chilly winds of fall returned to the forest. One of those days; two hunters came from under the bush. One of the hunters put his rifle against the Pole while he too leaned against the Telephone Pole and lit a cigarette.

They chatted for a while till the hunter hand finished smoking. He dropped his lit cigarette into the grass. While the other hunter yelled at him for doing such a stupid thing. Then two hunters disappeared back into the forest.

After the hunters left, the Pole got excited. "Now, I have something to tell the cables. Maybe now they will

think of me as important." The Pole was so happy that he ended up butting in into their conversation.

"I have got something to tell you!"

"This better be good," the cables said.

So excited was he telling the story of the two hunters who had leaned against him and had almost started a fire.

"You call that important? So, two hunters came and leaned against you, big deal!"

"Now, get out of here and leave us alone and I mean, never talk to us again."

The two hunters had now come back to their camp and lit a campfire nearby. They were cleaning their guns when a buck deer leaped into their camp site. Both men were startled. They quickly got their guns and ran after it.

While the hunters were out chasing the buck, a breeze came up and blew the ashes into the dry grass. The grass caught fire and kept spreading until it reached a dry tree. Instantly, it flamed up making the fire bigger. Soon their camp was on fire. The animals of the forest began to run for their life.

The commotion of animals running through the trees and the smell of wood burning made the Pole aware that there was danger

nearby. A bright glow in the near distance alarmed him all the more. What could he do? He first thought of warning the cables.

With good intentions and in spite of what he was told, he tried to warn the cables. But it was to no avail. They would not listen to him. In fact, they just ignored him.

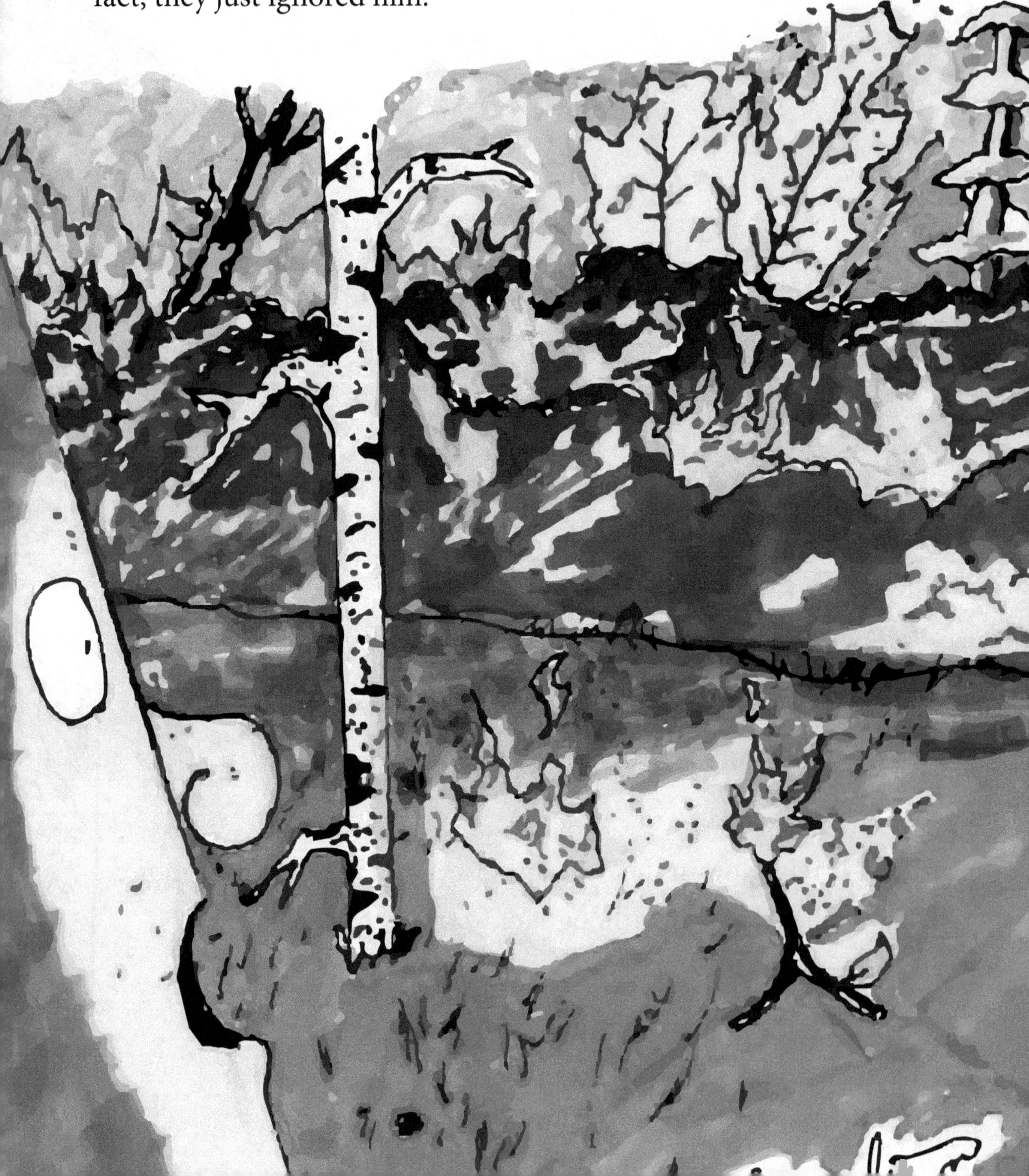

The Pole now alarmed at seeing the fire draw closer, ran up to the cables and cried out, "FIRE!"

By this time the cables were feeling the heat from the flames. The Pole lifted the cable as high as he could, away from the fires. All this time they all were screaming and giving instructions to him.

"Pole, lift me higher!"

"Ouch, the flames are burning my cover!"

"Pole, do something!"

"Why are you just standing there doing nothing?"

By now the fire was eating away at the Pole's sides. His hold on the cables began to weaken. Yet, the Telephone Pole was trying to protect them with all his might, even beyond his arms' reach. And the next thing he heard was a snap! He began to fall to the ground bringing the cables with him.

The Pole came crashing down to the ground with the cables still attached to his arms. Everything was burnt around him. The cables continued to be rude to the Pole.

"Why are you just lying down? How do you ever expect to be important just lying there?"

Another cable cried out, "Get us up from this dirty ground!"

"How do you think we're going to get messages lying here on the ground?"

"Pole! Pole! Do you hear us? We demand you lift us up there!"

It took them a while before they realized that he was not going to return them. At the same time they also realized, he was the most important of them all. For without the arms that held the cables high in the air no message would have gotten through.

All the four cables regretted being rude to the Pole. But now, it was too late.

The friendly Telephone Pole could not speak, no matter how hard the cables tried. It was too late but now they had learned a valuable lesson.

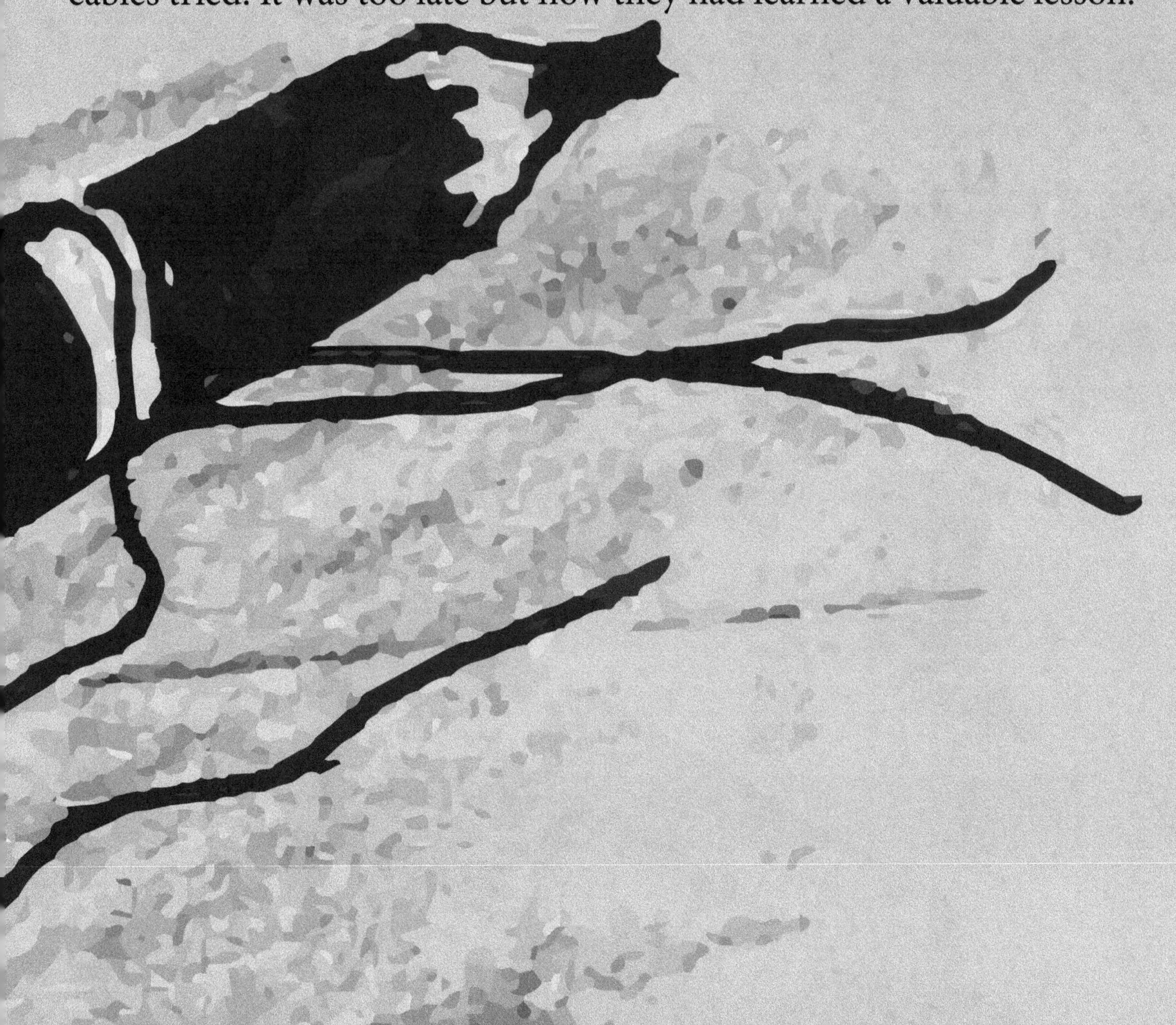

The Pole had been important all along holding those cables in place so that messages could get through to the outside world.

Days passed and soon the Pole was replaced with a new one. You can be sure that the cables treated our newcomer in a very friendly way.

SPECIAL THANKS

JUDY Williams

DORTHEY EVENHOUSE

LANCE SCOTT

JIMMY MARTIN

KEN GRAY

JEFF LYNCH

Cova Jean Brown